Teddy and the
Chinese Dragon

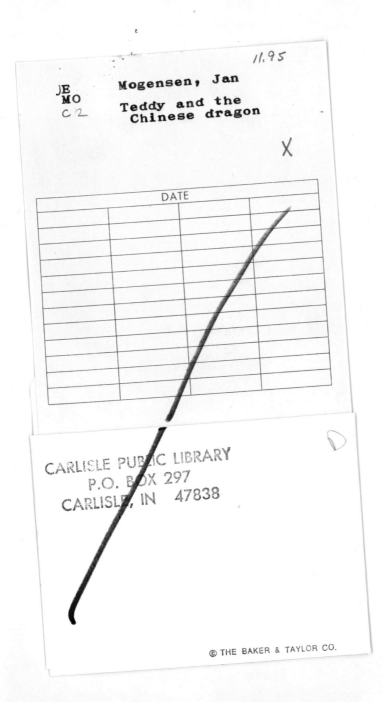

QUALITY TIME BOOKS™

TEDDY TALES:
Teddy in the Undersea Kingdom
Teddy's Christmas Gift
When Teddy Woke Early
Teddy and the Chinese Dragon

Library of Congress Cataloging-in-Publication Data

Mogensen, Jan.
   Teddy and the Chinese dragon.

   (Teddy tales) (Quality time books)
   Translation of: Bamse og den kinesiske prinsesse.
   Summary: While visiting a magical duck pond, Teddy overcomes his fear of
dragons with the help of his new friend, the Chinese Princess doll.
   [1. Teddy bears — Fiction. 2. Fear — Fiction. 3. Friendship — Fiction.
4. Dolls — Fiction] I. Title. II. Series.
PZ7.M7274Te   1985   [E]   85-26091
ISBN 1-55532-003-1
ISBN 1-55532-002-3 (lib. bdg.)

North American edition first published in 1985 by

Gareth Stevens, Inc.
7221 West Green Tree Road
Milwaukee, Wisconsin 53223, USA

First published as *Bamse og den kinesiske prinsesse* by Borgen with an original
text copyright by Jan Mogensen.

Typeset by Ries Graphics

English Text: MaryLee Knowlton

Teddy and the Chinese Dragon

Jan Mogensen

Gareth Stevens Publishing
Milwaukee

Max and Norah were going to the duck pond in the park.

Teddy rode in the red baby carriage. He was holding a bag of bread to feed to the ducks.

Teddy listened as Max told Norah a story. It was about a fierce dragon with sharp claws and teeth, and yellow eyes, and a long, fiery red tongue.

He tried not to feel scared, but to tell the truth, Teddy was a rather timid bear.

"We're going to feed the ducks, Teddy," said Norah.
"We'll be back soon."

She kissed Teddy and put him in his carriage. He watched
the ducks swimming around the island of the Chinese
pagoda.

Teddy felt himself growing sleepy. What had Max said
about the dragon? "Red eyes? Sharp tongue?" He was
getting confused.

Just then, a sudden noise made him sit up.

A porcupine stood at the foot of the carriage.

"A dragon!" screamed Teddy. And he leaped out of the carriage — head first into the pond!

Down through the water Teddy fell till, with a soft bump, he landed on the bottom of the pond.

"Help! Another dragon!" he yelled as he came eye to eye with a goldfish.

Suddenly Teddy felt a yank on his ear. Something pulled him back out of the water.

Now, Teddy knew a duck when he saw one, so he wasn't afraid.

"Thank you for saving me," he said to the duck. "I've just narrowly escaped from two dragons! I'm feeling a bit beside myself."

"Well, hold on to my tail feathers," said the kindly duck. "I'll pull you to land."

Teddy crawled up on a big rock. He sat down to think things over.

"Well, first of all," he thought, "I'm on the wrong side of the water. The baby carriage is over there."

He called to the duck for another ride, but the duck was far away. So he sat down to wait for Max and Norah.

"And second of all," Teddy thought, "my clothes are all wet."

Teddy took off his wet clothes. He hung them on long reeds to dry and sat down.

"Good afternoon," said a soft voice behind him.

Teddy turned and, to his surprise, he saw a Chinese Princess.

"I'm so pleased you came to visit," said the Princess. "Won't you stay for tea?"

"I'd love to," said Teddy, "but I'm not dressed for tea."

"Wait here," said the Chinese Princess. And she disappeared under a big leaf.

The Princess returned with a red jacket, a pair of yellow silk pants, and a Chinese straw hat.

Teddy put them on.

"Shall we go?" smiled the Chinese Princess.

"Certainly," said Teddy.

"I'm so glad you've come, Teddy," said the Princess. "Most people are afraid of my dragon."

"Oh, dragon?" said Teddy, trying to stay calm. "You have a dragon, do you?"

"You're not afraid, too, are you?" asked the Princess.

"Of course not," Teddy said shakily. "But I think my clothes must be dry now. I should be going."

"Oh, please, come to tea!" said the Chinese Princess. "My dragon won't hurt you. Come and see, Teddy!"

The Princess led the way. As they came to a red gate, Teddy saw his third dragon of the day. And it was coming straight at him!

He threw himself to the ground. "Help!" he cried. "The dragon is after me already!"

"It's only a butterfly, Teddy," laughed the Princess. "Are you afraid of butterflies?"

"I'm afraid of everything!" Teddy cried.

"Then let's hold hands," said the Chinese Princess. "Holding someone's hand can help when things are new and strange."

Hand in hand the two friends approached the dragon.

"It's a statue!" said Teddy.

"Of, course," said the Chinese Princess. "Didn't you know?"

"Sure," said Teddy. "I knew that. It won't move, will it?"

"No," smiled the Princess. "Come closer."

"Oh, dear," said Teddy as they got close to the dragon. "He is in sad shape."

"Yes," said the Princess. "The weather is hard on him and he needs some repairs. A coat of paint would help, too."

"He should have his teeth brushed, too!" said Teddy.

They both laughed.

"Let's have tea!" said the Chinese Princess.

"This is lovely tea," said Teddy politely. "I've never had tea before. Max and Norah and I drink hot chocolate."

"Hot chocolate?" said the Chinese Princess. "I've never tasted that."

"Then come home with me!" said Teddy. "We'll have some this afternoon."

Back at the big rock, Teddy changed
into his own clothes. He hung the
red jacket, the yellow silk pants, and
the Chinese straw hat on a branch.

"May we have a ride to the other side?"
Teddy asked a passing swan.

"My pleasure," nodded
the swan serenely.

So Teddy and the Chinese Princess
settled into the soft white feathers
and floated slowly across the water.

Max and Norah came back. They found the Chinese Princess next to Teddy in the baby carriage.

"Look, Norah!" said Max excitedly. "A Chinese Princess doll is sitting next to Teddy!"

"Let's take her home," said Norah. "She will be a good friend for Teddy. We can all have some hot chocolate."

"Good idea!" said Max. "Tomorrow let's bring them to see the dragon on the island. I hope they're not too scared!"

Teddy and the Chinese Princess smiled to themselves.